# THE CHRISTMAS TEDDY BEAR

*Illustrated
by Ivan Gantschev
Adapted
by Andrew Clements*

PICTURE·BOOK·STUDIO · Neugebauer Press

Ellen and her mother arrived to visit Grandma and Grandpa two days
before Christmas.
Grandpa met them at the station and bundled them up in the sled.
It took almost an hour to get from the town out to the big estate,
but there was no hurry, and there was plenty to talk about.

Ellen loved arriving at Butterfield. She felt like the grand-daughter
of a king whenever she came to visit.
Grandpa always said, "Now remember Ellie, I'm just the caretaker here."
But that didn't matter to her.

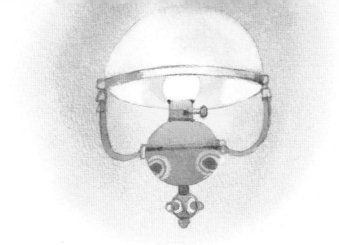

The caretaker's cottage was full of Christmas smell
a bowl of oranges on the table in the hall, the fir tr
in the parlour, and a plum pudding in the kitchen
Ellen gave her grandmother a big hug and then
took a long ride on the rocking horse Grandpa ha
made for her two years ago. There was no room
for it in their apartment in the city, so Ellen rode it
when she came to visit. Grandma said, "I keep it h
in the kitchen so I can think about you every day."

Ellen went to bed early, and she finished saying her prayers, she kept her eyes closed and whispered "Goodnight, Bear. I hope I see you on Christmas morning."

The next morning, Grandma was out of sugar, so Grandpa got on his coat. He asked, "Do we need anything else from town?" Mother needed some thread, and then she said, "Will you see if you can find a teddy bear for Ellen? I know it's what she wants, but when I went to buy one, the toy shop had none left." Grandpa laughed. "You leave it to me. If there's a teddy bear anywhere in town, I'll find it."

On the long walk to town, Grandpa thought about all the Christmas mornings he had seen in his life – more than seventy! And he could still remember so clearly the time when his own mother and father had given him a teddy bear. He could see that bear's black shiny eyes, and the bright red hat his mother had put on its head. He chuckled and thought, "Yes, there's nothing quite like a new teddy bear."

Everyone in town was bustling about, and Grandpa bustled, too. He bought the sugar at the grocery, the thread at the button shop, and best of all, he found a nice big teddy bear at the toy shop. Then, just for fun, he bought a bright red cap and pulled it onto the bear's head. With all his errands done, he ate a little lunch and then headed for home.

Grandpa had been walking only a little while
when it started to snow.
At first it was just a few flakes, but soon the snow
was coming hard and fast, and the wind was
getting stronger by the minute.

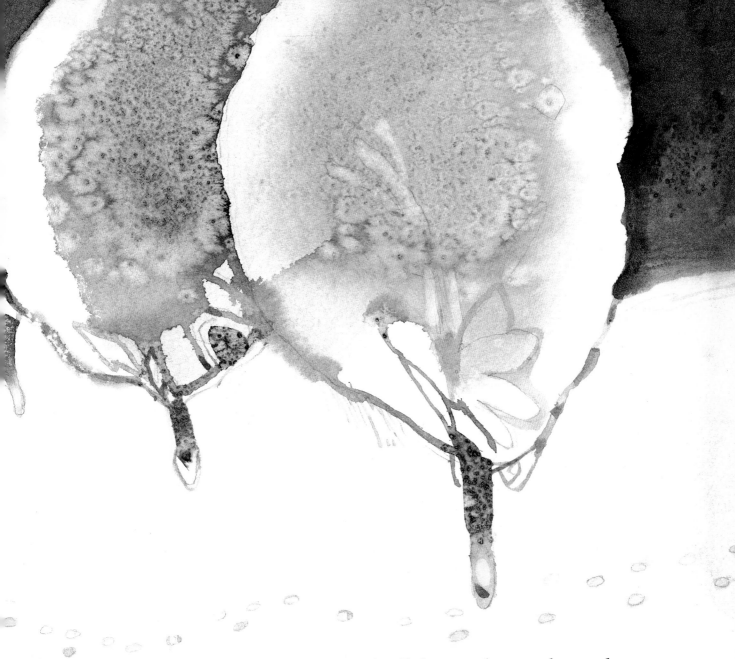

By the time Grandpa had turned off the road onto the path
through the woods, it was snowing so hard that his footprints
were filled in and covered up almost before he took the next step.
The whipping wind and the blowing snow made it hard to see.
Before long Grandpa was lost.

It started to get dark, and Grandpa still had not returned. Grandma was worried, so she asked their neighbours for help. They brought their lanterns and went out to search for Grandpa. Ellen's job was to ring the bell at the chapel so Grandpa could hear it and know which way to walk through the storm.

Everyone searched for almost two hours.
It was getting very dark, and as the snow stopped,
it began to get colder.
They needed to find Grandpa soon.

Suddenly, just at the edge of the lantern light.
The gardener thought he saw something – something red!

It was the teddy bear's hat, and in the snow
underneath was Grandpa, very cold, but still alive.

They helped him up, and together they walked
toward the sound of the chapel bell.

A short while later, Grandpa was in bed sipping hot soup. Ellen was in bed too, for she had become very cold and tired from ringing the bell. Her mother had tried to make her come down, but she had stayed there until Grandpa was back safe and sound.

Everyone
fell asleep early,
all except one damp little teddy bear.
He sat near the fir tree all night long with his shiny eyes wide open,
waiting for a wonderful Christmas day.

Ask your bookseller for these other Picture Book Studio books
illustrated by Ivan Gantschev:
THE TRAIN TO GRANDMA'S
NOAH & THE ARK & THE ANIMALS
THE CHRISTMAS STORY BY FATHER CHRISTMAS
GOOD MORNING, GOOD NIGHT
THE MOONLAKE
WHERE IS MR. MOLE?
TWO ISLANDS
JOURNEY OF THE STORKS
A DAY IN THE LIFE OF BIG BERT
CANOEING
FILIO, THE TREE